T0195846

The Mount Rushmore Camping Adventures of the 4 Weiner Doggies -

PEANUT, BUTTER, JELLY, AND HONEY

JAMES STERN

To order additional copies of this book, contact:
Xlibris
844-714-8691
www.Xlibris.com
Orders@Xlibris.com

ISBN: 979-8-3694-0593-2 (sc)
ISBN: 979-8-3694-0592-5 (e)

Print information available on the last page

Rev. date: 08/21/2023

The Mount Rushmore Camping Adventures of the 4 Weiner Doggies -

Peanut, Butter, Jelly, and Honey

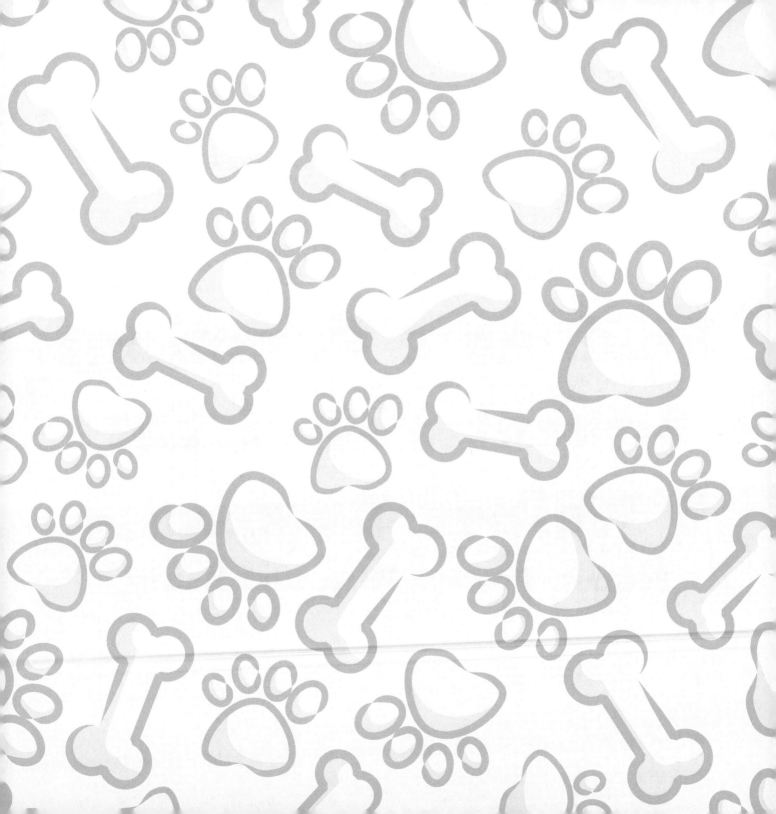

Chapter I

Peanut, Butter, Jelly, and Honey are looking forward to their camping adventure in Mount Rushmore. They want to go hiking, fishing, canoeing, horse riding, and play with new friends that they meet. And, Honey also wants to play Hide N Seek with Deer in the forest - Silly Honey!

Chapter II

Peanut, Butter, Jelly, and Honey are at home packing for their camping trip. Peanut packs lots of blankets, Butter packs lots of food, Jelly packs lots of candy, and Honey packs her nightgown, bathrobe, and slippers - Silly Honey!

Chapter III

When Peanut, Butter, Jelly, and Honey arrive at their campground, they are super hungry after the long drive! Peanut wants to eat popcorn, Butter wants to eat potato chips, Jelly wants to eat chocolate candy, and Honey wants to eat a steak and baked potato - Silly Honey

Chapter IV

Peanut, Butter, Jelly, and Honey meet their camping guide, Mr. Moose. Mr. Moose will cook a delicious dinner for Peanut, Butter, Jelly, and Honey. Mr. Moose is so nice to the girls! He also wants to bake a nice cake for their dessert. When Honey hears about the dessert, she tells Mr. Moose to bake a chocolate cake with chocolate ice cream - Silly Honey

Chapter V

It's bedtime for Peanut, Butter, Jelly, and Honey and the Tents and sleeping bags look so comfortable. Peanut likes to sleep with her teddy bear, Butter likes to sleep with her barbie doll, Jelly like to sleep with a snack, and Honey likes to sleep with her IPHONE and IPAD - Silly Honey

Chapter VI

As the sun rises over the campground, Peanut, Butter, Jelly, and Honey want to go hiking today. As the girls put on their hiking boots and get ready for a fun hike, Honey wants to drink a Hot Chocolate with whipped cream and marshmallows before the hike - Silly Honey

Chapter VII

Peanut, Butter, Jelly, and Honey want to play Hide N Seek with their new friends Debbie Deer, Samantha Squirrel, and Bella Bear. They love their new camping friends! They love playing games with their new friends on the campground. Butter wants to connect with everyone on Facebook so they can meet again! Honey says she will handle all the Social Media Apps from her IPHONE and IPAD - Silly Honey

Chapter VIII

Peanut, Butter, Jelly, and Honey want to go canoeing and fishing today. The girls are very hungry and want to catch some yummy trout fish. Not too many fish were caught on the fishing trip, but Honey decided to go to a fish market and buy lots of fish for dinner - Silly Honey

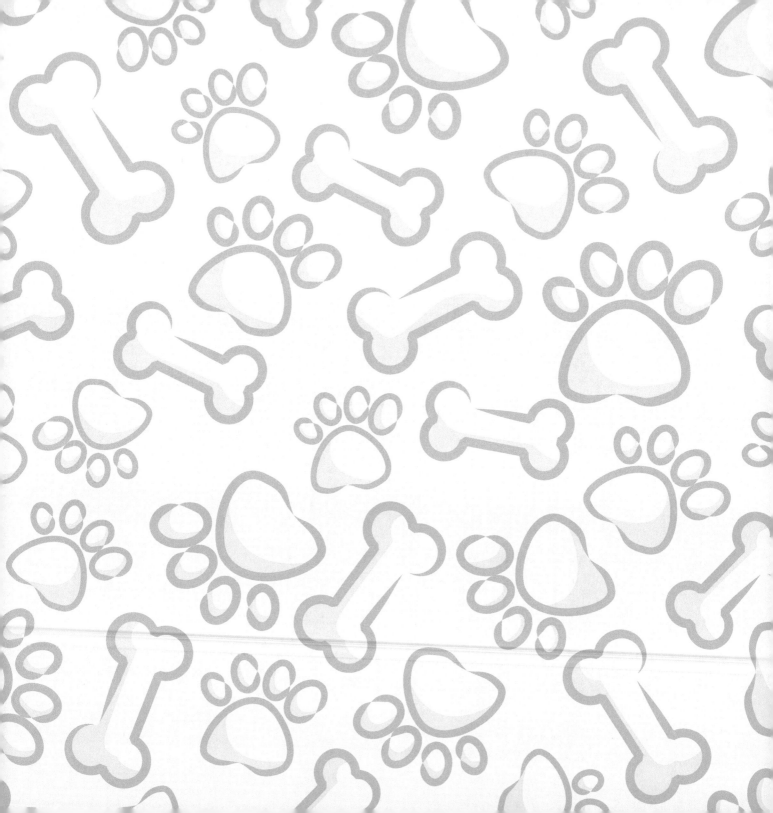

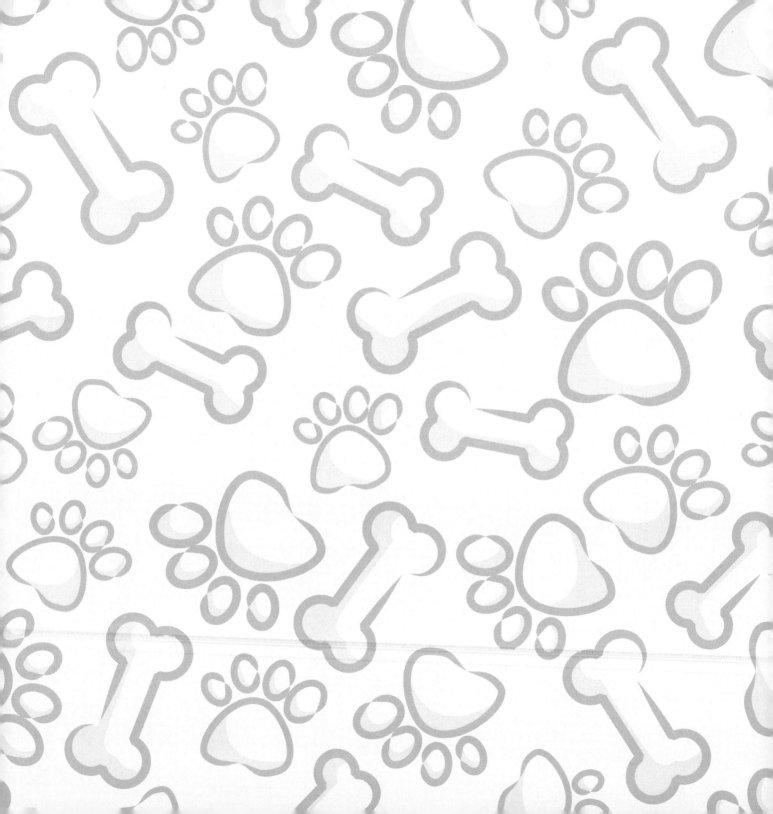

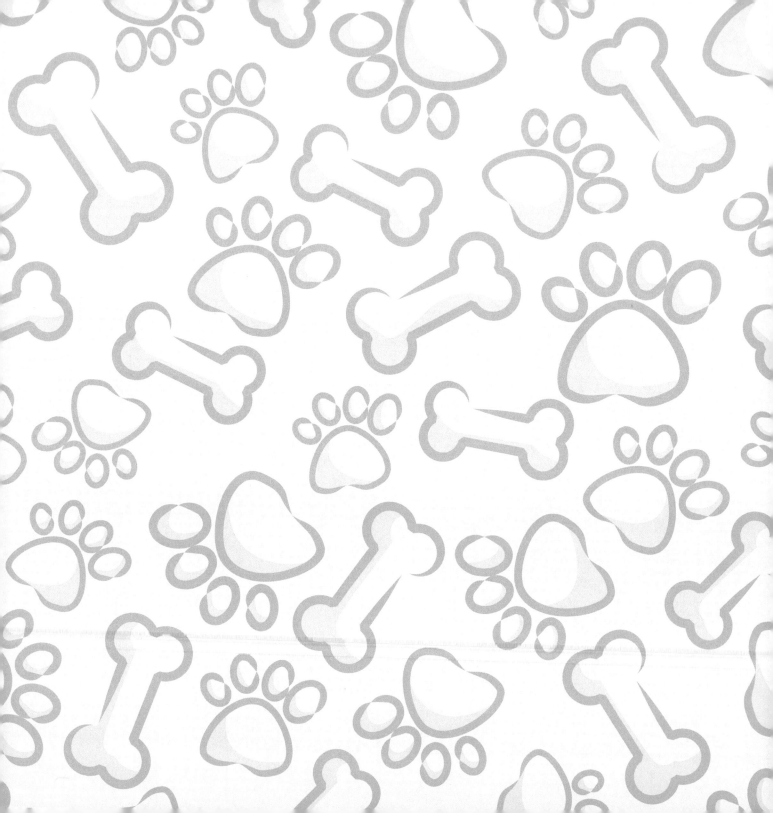

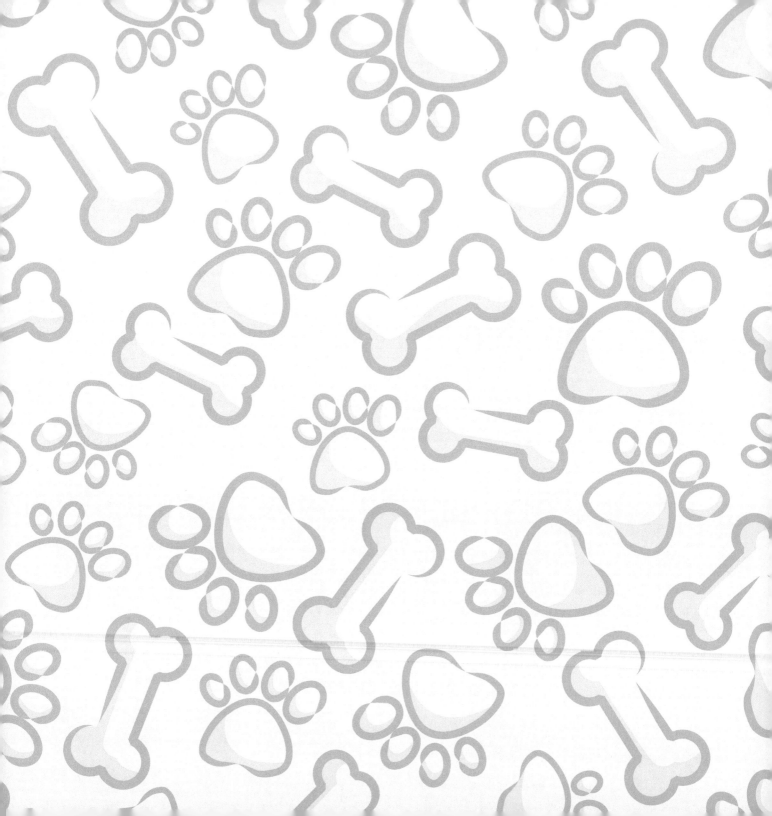

Printed in the United States
by Baker & Taylor Publisher Services